10 Short Stories

Wayne Campbell Reid

© Wayne Campbell Reid 2012

All rights reserved

No part of this publication may be reproduced, stored in a retrieval system, or transmitted in any form or by any means, without the prior permission in writing of the publisher, nor be otherwise circulated in any form of binding or cover other than that in which it is published and without a similar condition including this condition being imposed on the subsequent purchaser.

First published in Great Britain

All paper used in the printing of this book has been made from wood grown in managed, sustainable forests.

ISBN13: 978-1-78003-399-0

Printed and bound in the UK
Pen Press is an imprint of
Indepenpress Publishing Limited
25 Eastern Place
Brighton
BN2 1GJ

A catalogue record of this book is available from the British Library

Cover design by Jacqueline Abromeit

Contents

Introduction

Part 1 - Romantic poems and love songs   1

  I love you   3

  Father Christmas   4

  The highway of the lord   5

  Heaven sent   6

  Diana, the hunter of the lamb   7

  The peacocks cry   8

  Magic love and potions   9

  You are the only one for me babe   10

  Like the moment of life   11

  Heaven is yours   12

  Grace   13

  Falling snow, merry laughter   14

  I'm sorry for what they did   15

  Watching over me   16

Still remains a mystery to me	17
Mr Coalman	18
Rainbow girl	19
I've cried for so many years	20
Feel	21
Unicorns drinking by the river	22
Thunder and lightning	23
Clear water and palm trees	24
Part 2 - love letters to god	25
1997	26
Sentimental thoughts	29
The bird of prey	31
The angel Knight	32
Na na da da na na dad Dad	33
The all Seeing Eye	34
The golden fairy wizard	35
Billy and his X-box	37
Billy and the lost shoe	39
20 rules to live by	41
About the author	42

INTRODUCTION

This is a book of ten short stories. Book 1, is a collection of love songs and poems. Book 2, is like a grail of prayer that would make a good opera or ballet. Book 3, is a life circle of a pair of eagles. Book 4, is a short song about the taxman. Book 5, is a book about the all Seeing Eye. Boo 6, is a sort of fairy tale. Book 7, is about a boy who gets an X-box for Christmas. Book 8, is a book on common sense. Book 9, is about a boy that loses his shoes. Book 10, is about the angel night.

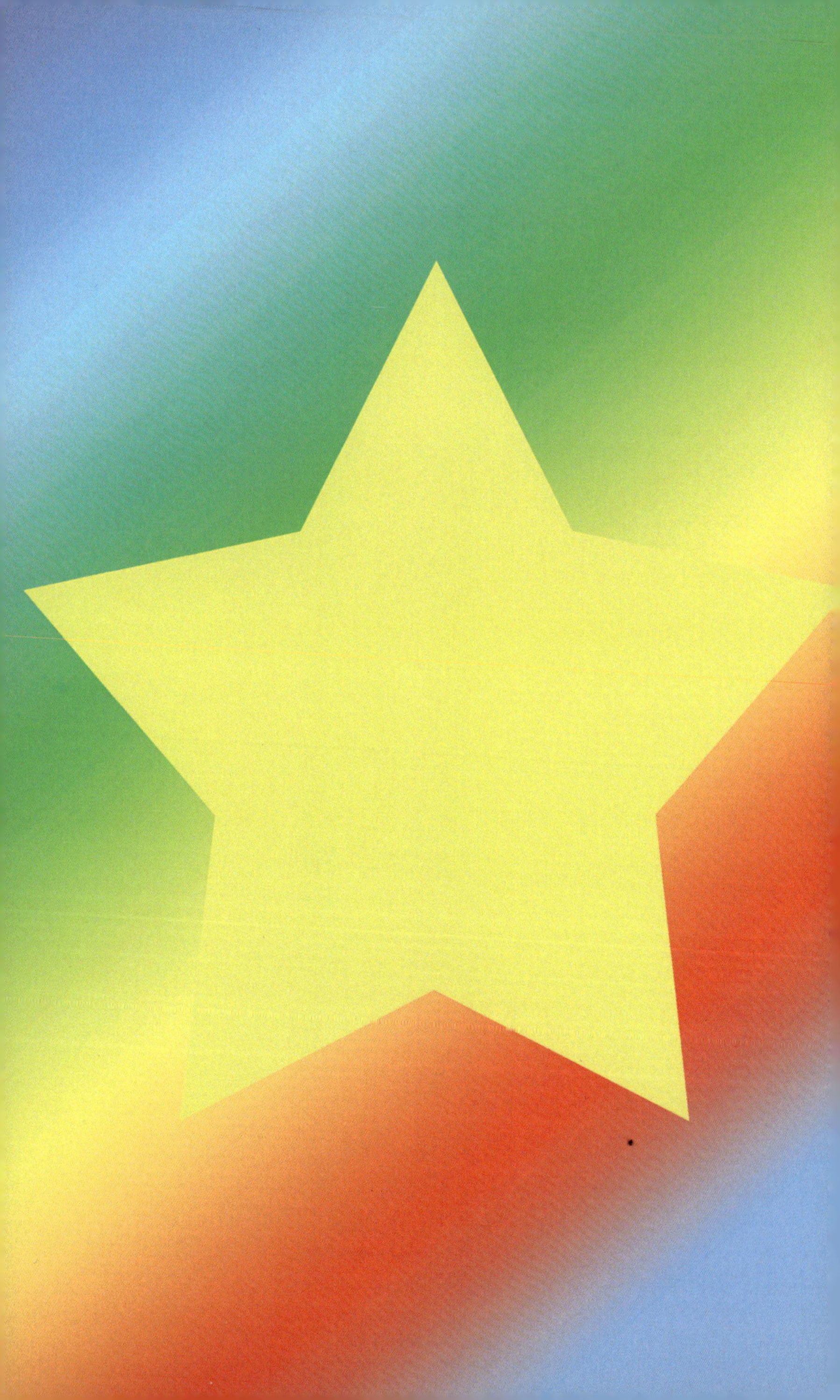

Shining heavens-heavens sent

ROMANTIC POEMS AND LOVE SONGS

By

Wayne Campbell Reid

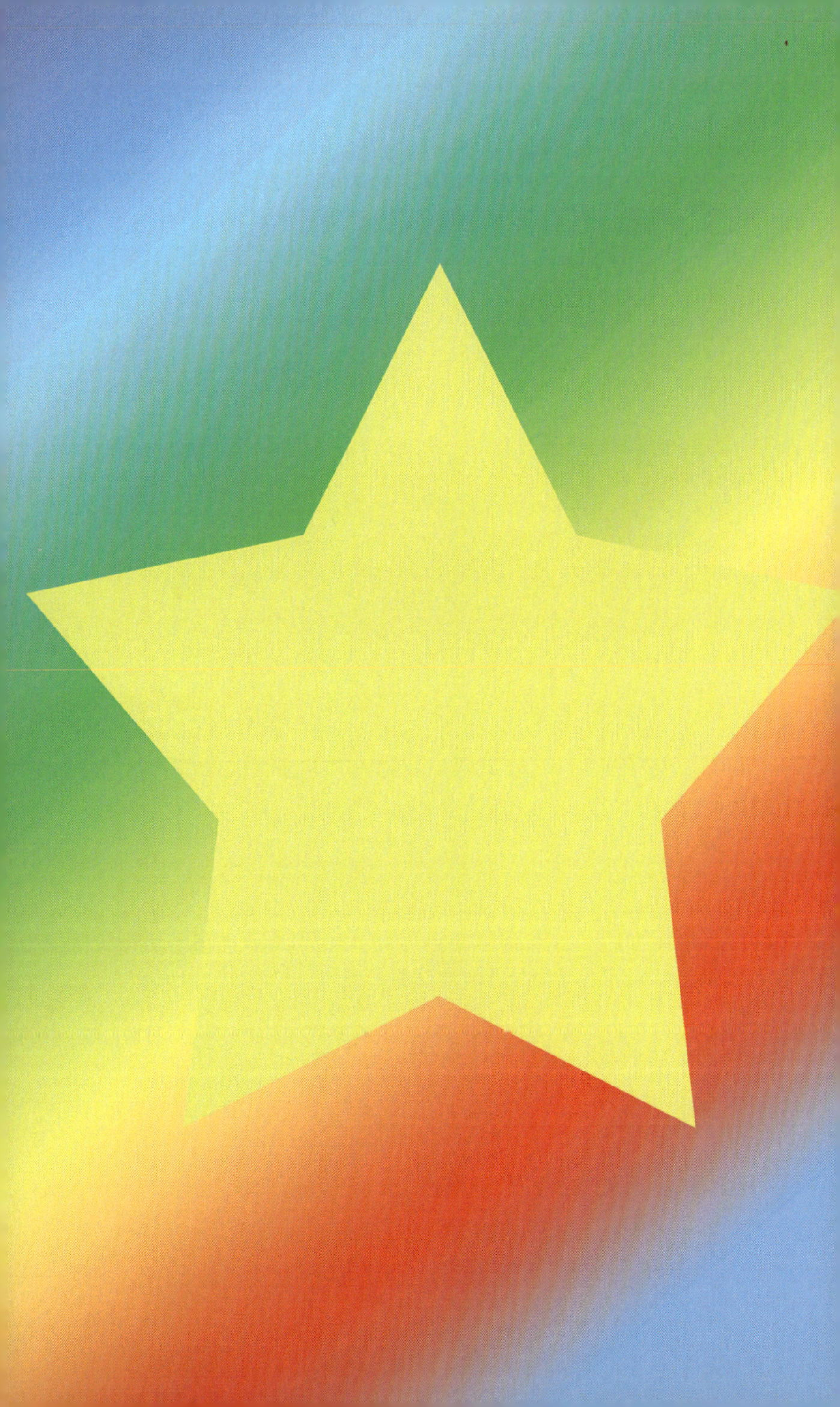

I Love You

Even though I love you, just like riding in a limousine

Oh! I want to be alone now because you've hurt me so badly, even though you're greatest pain in my life,

And I still love you. Oh! I will come back one day, and take you away with me. I call to the heavens above for your love, like the grass grows and rain falls, so fish can swim under the waterfall.

As the rainbow shines in the sky, and birds can drink from the side pool, and fairies play, as the butterfly flutters to the harmony of our love, and flowers grow. Ships sail into the horizon, as the sun sets in the sky, and seagulls fly and mermaids sing to Neptune.

'What a heavenly world there is for us'

Oh I will do anything for you. Try and understand that I love you. Because of this, like chariots of fire in the sky, taking us for a ride in the heavens above.

Oh I love you, like riding in a big white limousine.

Father Christmas

Oh Father Christmas, hear my plea from the ends of the earth people join me! Hoping and expecting to shower us with presents, boys and girls looking at the fireplace eager and tense. As his sleigh is pulled swiftly through the night sky, mortals laugh and drink your health merrily. Your white beard glows in the moonlight. Dropping great presents, small and big in your chimney! Snowflakes dropping setting the scene night air is chilly but clear!

Clean is the land in a blanket of snow! On this significant day. Oh Father Christmas, hear my plea lighting up my life like a Christmas tree! Stoke up the fire, as he's coming smiling as he flies by in the clouds. Wipe those tears away for love is here on this special day! Children playing with the snowmen and throwing snowballs!

The highway of the lord

Golden alter, woven with an unbelievable vine, oh I'm dead excited now. Give us a ride in your big flash, flash sports car, and let's hit the highway, passing everything by. Hear that engine run tyres gliding on the floor, like a dream machine, or even a ride in your space ship. Heavens and galaxies of wonderful lands. Passing by. All I really want to hear is you won't believe me down here, or give us a swan that lays golden eggs, flying in the sunset, into my hands. A golden alter woven with an unbelievable vine. Oh I'm dead excited now, give me a ride in you big flash fast sports car, and let's hit the highway, passing everything by. Hear that engine run, tyres gliding by. Hear that engine run, tyres gliding on floor, like a dream machine. A golden alter with an unbelievable vine, wishing for all these things.

Well you can only try. Oh I will. There's no looking back with me, and I know you're not taking me back. Because of the perfection in me. What a dream this is to me.

Heaven sent

I know you were heaven sent for me. I'm no fool, I believe in you. Like fields full of gold corn and maize, as the windmill goes round. You are the bread of life and eternal youth. Things we look at can also be changed if we use a telescope – or even look through a tube of card! They are framed in a circle – a swan, a flower, ice on sight this to me.

I wonder what you see. It's like everlasting light as the dragonfly flies by, or the brightness of sunflowers in the summer sun. It all means the same to me. I know you were heaven sent for me. I'm no fool, I believe in you. Like fields full of gold corn and maize, as the windmill goes round. You are the bread of life to me, giving me everlasting life and eternal youth and the heavens shine on me. Oh I am always sympathetic with you. It's alright, I understand, there's no need to be shy with me. So give us a kiss and say you love me. Now that's heaven sent.

Diane, the hunter of the lamb.

Diane, the hunter of the lamb, a saint maybe, I don't know! You're perfection to me. Everybody knows what you mean to me. As you arch your bow of love across the nation, what a wonderful thing you have done you can't ever imagine. What magnificent wonder you are. Try and understand. Because of this there will be a mighty heavenly place in heaven for you. Don't stop now; I told you, listen to the wind whispering through the leaves on the trees to show you the way. Please believe, there's even a golden tress for you, full of ripe, delicious fruit you can't even imagine for you.

Diane, the hunger of the lamb, a saint maybe, I don't know. You're perfection to me. Everybody knows what you mean to me. As you arch your bow of love across the nation, what a wonderful thing you have done for us. What a magnificent wonder you are. Try to understand because of this there is a mighty heavenly place in heaven for you, and on this lamb. I'm sure he's heard my prayers for you, babe!

The peacock's cry

As I stand in the castle grounds, as the peacock's cries to the illumination of the morning sunrise, and the ghostly monk walks the land with his incense, and the deer come close by, and horses canter in the fields, I play with the magical friendly dragon. What a game we played, looking at the whiten lady painted on the wall as the peacock opens its feathers to the illumination of the morning sunrise and I tell the tourist there's a dragon in the swamps. Well, the tourist came from everywhere. What a laugh that was. As I stand in the castle grounds, as I stand in the castle grounds, as the peacock cries to the illumination of the morning sunrise, and spreads his feathers, what a wonderful sight this is, and the ghostly monk walks the land with his incense, and the deer come close by, and the horses canter in the fields. I play with the magical friendly dragon. What a game we played, looking at the white lady painted on the wall, as the peacock cries to its other birdy friends, and the mushrooms grow so pixies can play too, and giants play with the giant stones.

Magic love and potions

Listening to the words you whisper in my ears, my magic love and potions are all yours. Oh you know I'm still free and you know there's no excuse for not seeing me, and turning your back on me because I know you are still free, free as a bird flying in the sky. Please believe in me, o yeah, believe. Can you hear my heart beating as you get closer to me? I'm telling you. I'm still free and there's no excuse for turning your back on me because I'm still free as a bird, flying in the sky. So please believe in me, and whisper sweet nothings to me. You are all I've got in my mind. My magic love and potions are all yours. Listen to my heart beating as you get close to me. There are excuses for turning your back on me. Now don't hesitate to show me your love girl, as the wind blows through the leaves on the trees.

You are the only one for me babe

You are the only one for me babe. What a marvellous feeling this is for me and you. Laughter and fun, passion we had, as you put your body close to mine, putting my hands through your golden woven hair, on the beach, under the palm trees, listening to the waves coming in on the seashore. You are the only one for me babe. Can you feel my body popping to the move? You make me feel so special. You are a heavenly queen to me. What marvellous feeling this is for me and you. Laughter, fun and passion we had, as you put your body close to mine, putting my hands through your golden woven hair, on the beach under the palm trees, listening to the waves coming in on the seashore, you are the only one for me babe.

Like the moment of life

Like the moment of life, you are the greatest pain of my life, my son. As I made you a garden of paradise, you mean everything to me. Visible boundaries there will never be between me and you. For I am always there in the garden and world to be, death to me would be a resurrection of life. Power and might is all yours my son. You will never be blind to things of this world, like the moment of life I've given you, and the garden of paradise I've shown you. As you mean everything to me. Visible boundaries there will never be between you and me. Essences of holy things will always be for you, and power and might is all yours. You will never be blind to the things of this world as you mean everything to me.

Heaven is yours

Heaven is yours, I know you are ready. I sent a message for you, I hope you received it. I even made a little tune as I want to play to you, for all the money in the world, you can buy me. Oh I'm so hard to get, yet you're so easy, take me to the moon and back and sing to me. As I'm going to rock the heavens, twinkling stars. What an orchestra I've got when God sings to me, and I sing to him. I made everything for you. I sent a message for you. I hope you received it. I even made a little tune, as I want to play to you. For all the money in the world, you cannot buy me. Oh I'm so hard to get, yet you're so easy. Take me to the moon and back, as I'm going to rock the heavens, and the phoenix roar to the kings.

Grace

As I cry at the mountain top for grace, harmony and love, oh why you have me like this! as I watch the planes go by, oh I want to fly, like riding in an aeroplane in the sky, it's time you were with me as the stars twinkle in the sky, sending little messages, saying I love you. Oh you make me feel like a king, with heavenly things, open your eyes, and look what I've found. Grace does this mean harmony and love for us, as I cry at the mountain tops for your grace of love, as I watch planes go by. Oh I want to fly, like riding in an aeroplane in the sky, as the stars twinkle in the sky, sending little messages, I love you. Oh you make me feel like I want to sing for joy.

Falling snow, merry laughter

Falling snow, merry laughter. My tears flow as I wake up alone. Spring, summer, autumn, winter. All year to this day, I miss your warmth. I stand alone in the mist of happiness. What did I do wrong? Maybe love should be all year round, not only for this day. I should learn from the king who was born on this day. Who loved and died for the whole world. But the best gift I have for you is that I believe in you! Never leave it for one day! Never leave it for one day! Love your brother and sister. Give praise to him constantly. Always remember the good times. Seek him. Seek him. Falling snow, merry laughter. My tears flow as I wake up alone. Spring, summer, autumn, winter. All year to this day, I miss your warmth. I stand alone in the mist of happiness. What did I do wrong! Maybe love should be all year round, not only for this day! I should learn from the king who was born on this day. Who loved and died for the whole world, but the best gift I have for you.

I'm sorry for what they did

I came all the way up there to find you just to say hello and sorry for what they did, the king in his marble grave. I could feel your gracious spirit and guidance within me. How thrilled I was, then they put me in prison too, where an angel confronted me. I know you will have Justine, Heavenly father, on them. I sing with the angel's voice to please you my lord, king, Jehovah of the world. I came all the way up there to find you just to say hello and sorry for what they did to the king in his marble grave. I could feel his gracious spirit and guidance within me. How thrilled I was, then they put me in prison too. Where an angel confronted me, sent from the lord. I know you will have justice, Heavenly father. I sing with heavenly angel's voice to please you, my lord, king, Jehovah of the world and heavens.

Watching over me

For all the stars in the sky shinning on me, it means nothing to me. Unless you are there watching over me. When you're riding on the breeze you mean everything to me, all the good times we had and the loving tender care you gave me, yes you deserve to be in heaven above. I wait till one day I will stand next to you, one day again in the sky in that heavenly, palace of love and harmony. For all the stars in the sky shinning me at night, it means nothing to me unless you're watching over me. All the good times we had together and loving tender care you game me. Yes, you broke my heart when you left as you meant everything to me. As I watch the clouds go by in the sky, it means nothing to me, unless you are watching over me.

'I give you my eternal love'

I dream to the heavens about you, in that heavenly palace of love and harmony.

Oh take me away one day,

Still remains a mystery to me.

Oh do you understand why I sleep alone, waiting for you?

No friend understands, to lend a helping hand. You're the greatest pain I've ever known. I don't know how you can walk away as easily as you left. It remains a mystery to me. Don't you remember that you promised me that you'll come back? I say these things because I'm happy and I sing because I'm free in his eyes. You're everything to me. Oh I pick up the phone, and you're on the line to someone else. I wonder why. After the love I've shown you, and the things I've done for you. Oh do you understand why I sleep alone. Waiting for you? No friend understands to lend a helping hand. You're the great pain I've ever known yet it still remains a mystery to me.

Mr Coalman

Oh Mr Coalman. You've underground now just so you can warm the cockles of my heart. What a glow I've found in you, as you hold your lamp in the dark, just so I can get a glimpse of you. Oh you go d own and come up black as the ace of spades. I wonder if you know what you are doing, as you light a fire for the world. You give me warmth and happiness. Like Daddy bringing the coal around the back, and in the front door, at New Year to bring good luck just like wishing to find a goldmine. It's cold land snowing, what warmth I've found in you. Mr Coalman, let's sing auld Lang syne, and sing to the spirit of love. You've found a fire to the heavens as you hold your lamp up. Oh let's sing auld Lang syne to bring New Year in. Oh Mr Coalman, as the fire burns inside, like a miracle on the cold winter's night.

RAINBOW GIRL

Silky golden rainbows, girl, will always shine for you. I can see you dancing on the symphony of stars. Now hold me tight, loves the name of the game. I'm singing from inside and I want to be with you tonight. Wipe away my tears rainbow girl. I need you now, sing to me like a bewildering buttercup. Oh we're together now rainbow girl, dancing in a dream of illusion. The stars are shining for you, love's the name of the game and I want to be with you. I've not got all the time in the world, so hold me now. Sailing millions miles into your horizon of love. Don't break my heart, rainbow girl; many ministers heard our cry to the heavens, with burning desire of eternal love. Harmony is to your beautiful woven lace. Oh heaven is shining for you rainbow girl, with burning desire of eternal love.

I've cried for so many years

We have been together for so many years. We've cried together, and shed many tears, but I cannot resist you leaving me now, because we've been together for so long. For if we have to leave each other now, I guess it's for the best also, I will still think of you because of your wonderful smile, and twinkle in your eyes. When I am there lying in bed, will you please come back to me. I can't bear living without you and I have cried so many tears over the years, thinking about you because I really love you. I really love you my fairy-tale queen, as I see that twinkle in your eyes, and I know it's hard, and I'm sure you love me my fairy-tale queen, as I've cried for so many years, as you light up my life.

Feel

I really don't feel like talking on the phone, and I really don't feel like company at all. Ever since you went away baby, my whole life baby changed. Baby I lost you! I don't want to lie. I don't want to play. I don't want to take. I have nothing to say. I don't want to go. Forget the show. I can't go on like this knowing you are gone. I really don't feel like smiling anymore. I haven't had a bit of sleep at all. So I still love you just remember that! I don't want to talk. I have nothing to say. I don't want to go. Forget the show, how can I go on like this knowing you are gone?

Unicorns drinking by the river

Unicorns drinking by the river of eternal water and divine magic. As I swim through the jungle as the animals listen closely by waiting for their call, look at this place. It's like everlasting life. My eyes are filled with wonderful things. It makes me want to cry, tears of joy and happiness flow. Beautiful birds with luminous colours glowing, never seen before. Unicorns drinking by the river of eternal water, and divine magic. As I swing through the jungle, as the animals listening closely by, wait for the call, look at this place. It's like everlasting life. As the unicorns drink by the river of eternal water, and dive magic filled with joy and happiness. And I swing through the jungle of golden trees and leaves, like riding on a cloud in the breeze, as the unicorns drink at the river of eternal water and divine magic.

Thunder and lightning

Thunder and lightning strike the land. God's wrath is evident of an evil rite. Electrical storms in the sky, of enormous power over evil condemning and expelling the devil into hell. Giving no peace till he's gone. Oh God, you're my hero of the universe giving me peace of mind and rest to carry on with my work. In your will, I will be mighty happy, respected. Because he works within me, there is no confusion of my love for him. I may be a saintly angel one day because of this. Thunder and lightning strike the land. God's wrath is evident of an evil rite. Electrical storms in the sky of tremendous power over evil, condemning and expelling the devil into hell. Giving no peace till he's gone. Oh God, you're my hero of the worlds. Giving me peace of mind and rest to carry on with my work, in your will, I will be mighty happy, respected. Because he works within me, there is no confusion of my love for him. I may be a saintly angel one day because of this. Whoever you are, what I want is the highest! So damn this nation, universal king that you are. Overall, I am here. Bring your holy spirit on me!

Clear water and palm trees

Everyone loves you, I get jealous. Because I want you for myself. Sharing the city of paradise with clear water and palm trees, every time I try it's just enough for you.

Walking in your footsteps, what a wonderful pathway you've created for me. I'm a universal soldier of the heavens with an army of angels, archangels, and saints as I will never be alone on my own. Sailing in the sky trying to see the world below, can't you see I love you? Oh everybody loves you; I get so jealous, because I want you for myself. Sharing you in the city of paradise, with clear water and palm trees, every time I try it's just enough for you.

Walking in your footsteps, what a wonderful pathway you've created for me. I'm a universal soldier of the heavens with an army of angels, and archangels. I will wait till the end of time for you.

Part 2

Love letter to God

By

Wayne Nicholas Campbell Reid

1997

Isn't it beautiful me and you lord, love me like a king and I will love you like a queen. Your spirit is all over me, you say where have you been and I say I have been right by your side, forever my darling. Let me put my fingers through your beautiful hair.

Oh sing sweet nothing to me darling, your everything to me, I want you for a lifetime, don't let things ever come between us lord, if I was ever apart from you I would go crazy, don't leave me oh don't leave me God. You give me everything you can believe in me. And the Sheppard's watch the stars in heaven. I belong to you, treat me nice and with aspiration, for you are my forever friend. Knock on the door or window and I will answer the door. You support my life with faith love, higher and higher you lift me as my higher power is in God. Touch and heal me, cleanse me of my sins I drank from cup and eat your bread I say the word. I call on your discipline. Disciples, Arch angels and herald angels. I gave my life for eternity, I don't doubt your word, and I know he will come again.

Sometimes I wonder when I'm by your side if I am dreaming, you're the only thing I need Oh lord, because of your love. You're the divine life, loving and blessing me compassions never failing me, guarding my heart, You are always there, let's dance, grant me your mercy's, always knowing what is the best for me and you come first in my life, honouring me like I honour you, seeing me through the hard times, take me in your arms tonight. Love is the prevalence of beautiful things such as you, tear by tear; my love for you will never end for you. You are like a flower in the garden of paradise, entailing beauty, look no further feeling terrified, hoping you'll show mercy. I am here watching you, oh don't let you go away, like a bird in the sky searching for prey, oh stop mocking my love for the lord his always present and grace, may be up on me. This is how much you love me, please don't be shy with me and take me one step this way to my side, embrace with me passion; you are a gift from heaven. Glory is yours and mine, the glory of good always prevailing I want you, what a beautiful thing you are and don't let me down as the electric of the dawn covers the grass, what a wonder thing, that he's listening to the clock ticking and how peaceful this is, I stumbled and you pick me up, you make me feel so good, I need your time of sweet harmony as the angels sing to me you are my witness. I know you are there, to give and cherish. Success in decisions, you are heaven sent, no one fools you lord, Diana Ross, Tina Turner, Madonna, and Kylie, and the rest, you take me in for ecstasy all around the world, just say you love me. But I still hurt, I break like a heart, and you felt my wickedness end in hell.

Seen never before, the very eye. Just wait to explored, as I look to the galaxies, as the stars shine, listening for the slightest sound of like. Spaceships will watch and fly.

Mary where is he alive for him? His divine task and my row of hurting, the road like one of the good things in life is right in front of my eyes. Day and night comes, and I say Mr DG pump up the volume, putting another CD going through the heavens. She wiped the smile off my face, and you put it back on again, yet all I know, I will triumph my love never ends. I am waiting for the day, that I will have a family and be in comfort and stable. Oh lord I pray sometimes I wonder when I'm by your side if I am dreaming, you're the only thing I need oh lord, because of your love. You're the divine life, loving and blessing me, compassions never failing me, guarding my heart, You are always there, let's dance, grant me your mercy's always knowing what is the best for me and you come first in my life, honouring me like I honour you, seeing me through the hard times, take me in your arms tonight. Love is the prevalence of beautiful things such as you, tear by tear; my love for you will never end for you. You are like a flower in the garden of paradise, entailing beauty, look no further feeling terrified, hoping you'll show mercy. I am here watching you; oh don't let you go away, like a bird in the sky searching for prey. Oh stop mocking my love for the lord is always present an grace, may be up on me. This is how much you love me please don't be shy with me and take me one step this way to my side, embrace with me passion; you are a gift from heaven. Glory is yours and mine, the glory of good always prevailing I want you, what a beautiful thing you are and don't let me down as the electric of the dawn covers the grass what a wonderful thing, that he's listening to the clock ticking and for this, hear my words and know that I'm here, that you holy spirit be on me. Oh let's be fruitful and multiply. I had a vision of you, so bliss and wonderful, I'm held by the spirit; his wisdom makes me wine and gives me the breathing life.

By you all things were created, you knew me before I was even born. I was born blind and you made me see, to a whole multiple of things and I am so grateful. I will never stop my love for you, your generosity never fails, when I trust in you, cleanliness is a sign of godliness. You fill the fountains and the mountain stream and the grass grows and the cattle graze, surely this must be a sign of heavenly things, poetry at its best; it's like a miracle. No matter where you are I will be waiting for you. I hope there is peace of heart for my soul will go on to the gates of heaven and beyond. When will I see you again, I wait for this day. Peace and harmony is all yours. You're everything I need, peace be with you I thank you for everything I have and praise you, let's see the world sing and dance, with love you take the seed of life and create life compassion it's all yours. Giving me courage, I congratulate you for all the wonderful things you do. I call to you for guidance I can see.

Sentimental Thoughts

A Walk down Memory Lane

Take a walk down memory lane and see where a pac?? to my need. You are a million things to me but in our minds they stay the same. When I look at you instantly I get sentimental about you. When you're holding my hand walking through the park, it seems like yesterday, it felt so good to be in love. Magnificent is what you are to me. Take a walk down memory lane and see where a pac my knee. You are a million things to me but in my mind they stay the same. When I look at you instantly I get sentimental about when you're holding my hand. Walking through the park, it seems like yesterday, it felt so good to be in love. Magnificent is what you are to me

I watch the stars at night for sign of life, seeing the old man cuddled up the fire on the street, and wondering why, let's hope he'll find his way and a dry and clean place to stay and people in shelters find a home, and their hunger and thirst is quenched. Heal their broken hearts day and night was one of your desires a bunch of flowers, for you and to get the rose of the lot. Let's have a banquet to feed the poor, and let them all come together for God is good.

Just let there be no more abuse and cruelty in the sight of the living and believe there is good and bad which you do, choose to be. Clarification leads to the declaration, it's up to you, what you do but you will be judged, whichever way you go for there will be justice in the end no matter what, depending if you said sorry or you carry on sinning for God's word is his word.

I sit and eat because I believe in the lord sent this a wonderful thing, and I am truly thankful and should you for the path of the lord is the right way, which path are you going down?

What great joy to follow him, fears can be rewardful, ships sail in the horizon as the sun sets in the sky and seagulls fly, and mermaids sing. She likes fire in the palm of your hand. I say I got up that morning like the burning bush, I live in fear, but I listen to the stars like fireworks in the sky. Business and unemployment blooming and welfare are created.

The clouds in the sky are like a river of life creating and destroying. May the good angels look after you and me! Hoping you're the only thing in my life! Through the traffic light, turning left and right and I'm outside my house, get out of the car, open the front door and you're in, put the kettle on and make myself a cup of coffee and make myself something to eat, then I'm ready for another day. Turn on the radio and begin resting on the lords day, give to those that believe and healing.

I stay fit and healthy in the lord as it is the right way, he wants you to live and look after yourself, graceful and majestic in your namemy rock, my strength, my weakness, my partner and my eternal, youth. That is my life you are my eternal life, broken down, tear after tear missing you, what am I going to do? My heart is unbelievably craving for you. I came into this world with nothing and I will leave with nothing, but I will know there will believe there is a heaven for me and I will be as grateful for this as I trust and believe in you. I hope you do because he loves you too. The high temples in the mountains and the skies are the paradise of the human race and the nature will never cease to end in your eternal gardens.

The ladies of the lake will live on and the sword will rise again, like a staff guarding the mountains.

The Bird of Prey

The eagle in the sky flies at speed with distinction and grace. The small birds fly and mice, and other rodents run with fear.

Summer comes and it's time to feather their nest and lay their eggs, the eggs hatch and they start to bring their young up and watching carefully over them.

High away from anything. She sits so perfectly and with such precision.

Protecting her eggs. The male hunts for food.

The female stirs up the nest and hovers over them, the eagles grow until they are able to leave the nest. The eagles teach their young to fly and catch prey.

Soon they will leave their parents to lead their own lives, and in the next summer they will raise their own young. And the cycle will start again.

THE ANGEL KNIGHT

God love my soul while I'm alive on earth like the salvation of love with an eagle flying above. Let the angel knights love with a blossoming of bridges in glory, with a hail of saints. When you say you love me, I know you mean it. If you do this for me. Riding my love to the sunset knight, till death. What a passion I have for you gliding and wanting your love. Tell the bloom of the eclipse of the moon, till the sun shines in the morning. You are my dream lover, like the eagle flying above a dove! God love my soul while I'm alive on earth like the salvation of love.

Na Na Da Da Na Na Dad Dad

I've got the grove, hurry up and pay the taxman.

I've got the grove, I've paid the taxman.

Now the money is rolling in, and put you convictions.

Right, I've got the grove, I've got the grove.

Paid the taxman, hurry up and put your convictions right .

I've got the grove. The money is rolling in.

I've got the grove.

Na Na Da Da Na Na Dad Dad

The money's rolling!

The all Seeing Eye adventures in arcane realms

God is like the blue sky and the clouds.

Like the all Seeing Eye and the beauty of his love is all around

Like the stars in the sky are like the eyes of the angels.

Seeing everything and knowing everything.

Like the waves coming in on the seashore.

Things grow and human beings drink and eat.

Like a star itself and sometimes seeing like an all seeing eye

On earth being watched from heaven's and from below like gods

all Seeing Eye, and out of all the gods they all know the lord

Is supreme ruler of all them put together, and the most holiest

The golden fairy wizard

The golden fairy wizard had been locked away in a cave entrapped in a bottle for one hundred years, by the wicked goblin, with the golden fairy queen in the goblins cave. The goblin had sealed the bottle with a powerful spell. One day a leprechaun was walking on his travels, and notices a dark wood, and could sense something was wrong. He couldn't put his finger on it.

The sun was not shining and it was getting chilly out. Near the dark wood the leprechaun stumbled on a weary frog.

The frog was shaking with fear. The leprechaun said to the frog, 'What's the matter.'

The frog replied, 'The wicked goblin is going to eat me!'

The leprechaun said, 'Now, now. Don't worry I'll see what I can do.' Then the leprechaun said to the frog, 'What's the matter with the wood. There seems to be no life in it.'

The frog said, 'I'm too frightened to tell you,' and the frog was shaking with fear.

'Now now,' said again the leprechaun. 'Come on little frog it cannot be as bad as that.'

'It can be,' the frog said. 'Yes it is, the wicked goblin locked the fairy wizard and his queen away, in his cave. The golden fairy wizard and his queen give life to the wood. The goblin has cast a powerful spell on the seal on the bottle, of which they are in. The wood as no life and that's why the wood is like it is, where they use to live. It has been like that for one hundred years.'

The leprechaun confronted the frog and did some of his magic. The weary old frog soon perked up and was happy again. The leprechaun and the frog sat down. They both had something to eat and drink, as they were very hungry. The leprechaun said to the frog, 'I can do something about the golden fairy wizard and his queen.'

The frog perked up even more and was very happy. They both rest for a while. Then the leprechaun said to the frog, 'Show me where the golden fairy wizards are.'

They both set off to the cave; they trekked very carefully and quietly along the path next to the stream. When they got to the cave, there a big stone rolled across the front of the opening. They could hear the goblin groaning and moaning and stayed quietly as they could, just in case the wicked goblin heard them. The leprechaun did some kind of magic and the stone slowly rolled away from the entrance of the cave. They hurried into the cave and low and behold, there was the bottle containing the golden fairy wizard and queen. The leprechaun picked up the bottle and the leprechaun did a very powerful spell. All of a sudden the bottle top came off; the fairy wizards flew out of the bottle.

The wicked goblin had heard them and was running towards the cave. All of a sudden the wicked goblin turned to stone. The golden fairy wizards thanked the leprechaun and the frog very much. Then a rainbow filled the sky. The gold wizards lifted the leprechaun and the frog up and flew to the wood. As soon as they got the wood lit up and was filled with beautiful life again, and a rainbow shone over the golden wood. And two unicorns came out to drink by the stream. Well the leprechaun was very pleased with himself. The golden fairy wizards were free and the wicked goblin turned to stone. The wood was filled with beautiful life again. Then all of a sudden the weary frog turned into a beautiful princess and the leprechaun turned into a handsome prince. And they all lived happily ever after.

Billy and his X-box

Billy sat on the window ledge looking out at the night sky. The land was covered by a blanket of snow.

He started to wonder what Santa will bring him this year. Seeing if he could see Santa and his reindeer, but he could see no site of Santa. Billy's mum said to Billy, 'It's time to go to bed now Billy.'

Billy went to bed and said 'Good night' to his mother and father. Billy's mother and father gave him a good night kiss and said, 'You only have to wait till morning son and you'll be able to see what Santa as brought you.'

Billy soon went to sleep and low and behold there was a jingling of bells. It was Santa rested his reindeers on the roof top and went down the chimney with a sack of presents.

Billy's mother and father had left out mince pies and a drink for Santa. Santa put the presents at the bottom of the Christmas tree and sat down to eat his mince pies.

Santa drank his drink and ate his mince pie and off he went. Up the chimney and on his sledge and went on his way to deliver more presents. Everyone was fast asleep in the house. Soon it was morning and everybody awoke.

Billy got up and rushed down the stairs, where his mother and father were waiting for him. Low and behold the bottom of the Christmas tree was covered in presents. Billy didn't know what to do and was stuck for words. Billy's mum and dad was so happy to see Billy happy and said go on then, open your presents. Billy opened a present and it was a X-box 360. Billy said, 'WOW.'

Billy's mum and dad opened their presents, and between them they had all the games for the X-box. They all opened the rest of their presents and they had the new play station 3 and a Nintendo with all the games, they were all very pleased with what Santa brought them.

Billy and the lost shoe

Billy does not like curry.

Billy is a teenage boy

Billy's favourite saying is 'flipping heck'

Billy has a nice personality.

Billy's favourite food is beef sandwiches and salad.

Billy had been in school all day. He had a good day and was very pleased with himself. It was time to leave school. Billy got on the bus and gave the bus driver his fare, and sat next to a window. The bus driver drove off. It was only ten minutes before billy had to get off the bus, and billy began to get of the bus.

Billy said, 'thanks' to the bus driver. As billy got of the bus the doors of the bus closed and billy caught his shoe. The bus started to drive off. Billy was not hurt and ran after the bus and managed to catch up with the bus and stop it. The bus driver opened the doors and got out of his seat, and gave billy his shoe. The bus driver asked if he was ok. Billy said, 'yes thanks' and put his shoe back on. The bus driver got back in his seat and said, 'see you billy,' and drove off and he began to walk to his house.

When billy arrived home, he knocked on the door and his mother opened the door, billy then took his coat off and hung it up. Billy's mother was making tea and said, 'it's curry.'

Billy said, 'flipping heck.'

Billy's mother said, 'it's not really, it's your favourite meal.' And low and behold, it was beef sandwiches and salad.

Billy was really happy that he was getting his favourite meal, a nd low and behold when it was ready billy ate it all up and said, 'thanks to his mother.' Billy sat down and rested for the evening and watched the music channel on the television.

20 Rules to Live By

1. EAT HEALTHY MEALS.

2. ALWAYS PAY YOR TAXES.

3. DO NOT SMOKE.

4. DO NOT DRINK.

5. DO NOT USE DRUGS.

6. REMEMBER FOOTBALL IS JUST A GAME.

7. DO NOT USE GUNS.

8. KEEP EXCELLENT HYGIENE AT ALL TIMES.

9. DO NOT STEAL.

10. LEARN WHATEVER YOU CAN.

11. ALWAYS KEEP TO THE SPEED LIMIT.

12. EXERCISE REGULAR.

13. BE KIND TO ONE ANOTHER.

14. PUT RIGHT WHAT YOU HAVE DONE WRONG.

15. ENJOY YOURSELVES AND BE HAPPY.

16. DO NOT MIS-USE KNIVES.

17. DO NOT USE BAD LANAGUAGE.

18. DO NOT PLAY WITH FIRE.

19. DO NOT LIE.

20. TREAT YOUR PARENTS WITH DIGNITY.

ABOUT THE AUTHOR

Wayne Campbell Reid was born in Warrington and was also educated in there. He spent some time as a QE2 Chef. Later after his return he spent the rest of his days in Cheshire. He is a good-natured person with a funny sense of humour, which he hopes come out in his work.